Celebration Song

To Gianna and Lydia: JB
To my father: LB

PUFFIN BOOKS

Published by the Penguin Group
Penguin Books Ltd, 27 Wrights Lane, London W8 5TZ, England
Penguin Books USA Inc., 375 Hudson Street, New York, New York 10014, USA
Penguin Books Australia Ltd, Ringwood, Victoria, Australia
Penguin Books Canada Ltd, 10 Alcorn Avenue, Toronto, Ontario, Canada M4V 3B2
Penguin Books (NZ) Ltd, 182–190 Wairau Road, Auckland 10, New Zealand

Penguin Books Ltd, Registered Offices: Harmondsworth, Middlesex, England

First published by Hamish Hamilton Ltd 1994
Published in Puffin Books 1996
10 9 8 7 6 5 4 3 2 1

Celebration Song

WRITTEN BY
James
Berry

ILLUSTRATED BY
Louise
Brierley

PUFFIN BOOKS

Your born-day is a happening day.
And, one year old today,
All day, I feel a celebration.
Everywhere is alive in jubilation.
All, O, all say, welcome!

And little eyes on me
light up lights in me
in choral songs
in drums, flutes and cymbals
in a world praiseful and joyful.

Singing dogs bang tins.

Cows play violins.

Hounds dance with foxes.

Lions dance

Snakes and snakes

dance with mongooses.

Wind dances palm trees;
groups of children sing.
All the trees sway and swing.

Fields and fields of animals dance.

with lambs.

Elephants beat drums.

With only one reason
today, all out of season
flame trees blaze in blooms.

Your born-day is a happening day:
a caller with good news,
a day of celebration,
a day of jubilation.

But, baby, now – go to sleep.
Baby Jesus, go to sleep.
I'll tell you your own own story.
First – how you began.

You came here well announced.
In one year, you have caused
fears, visions, parables
and the calling of councils.

Long before your coming
we had strange happenings.
A mystery messenger said
you would come to stay;

I should be your mother;
I should name you, Jesus.
In silence, in wonder,
afraid to say yes
I knew I saw you, my Jesus.

You were born so very quietly
and so very very simply
laid in a cattle-feeding trough,
wrapped in plain cloth.
But, in a grand company
messengers with no address
announced you to shepherds.

The shepherds hurried hurried
from sheep they protected
to come and bow down
to the little baby found.

Then, knowing your secret fame,
wise men, three astrologers
from a far country, came,
guided by a star,
to let your eyes meet theirs.

And there, over our roof
the stopped star was the sign
to meet here and come in.

The visitors bowed down to you.
With their many respects
they gave you their gifts
and left you sleeping.

Your born-day is a happening day:
All day I feel a celebration,
everywhere alive in jubilation.

You tried to open my eyes yesterday when I dozed, not liking them closed.

Busy little hands troublesome
they try to grasp my mouth,
my nose, my eyes: I mock shout!

Animals, people, trees
all say: first child
we want you for GOD'S own child.

In the sea the fishes all dance—
big fish, small fish, striped fish, plain fish—
in a leaping out-and-in dance
in a leaping out-and-in dance
in one all-day together wish.

All birds fill the sky
singing, flying in display
crisscrossed, this way and that way.

Your born-day is a happening day:
a caller with good news,
a day of celebration,
a day of jubilation.

Your born-day makes bells ring,
makes children and choirs sing,
brings strangers from near and far,
makes me feel afraid
yet feel a joy without dread.

When you grow up, and a man,
what will happen, happen then?
What will happen, Jesus?
What will happen to you, me, us?

Yet, also, I ask this:
When your childhood has gone—
my mothering long done—
will your day still be one
long long celebration day?

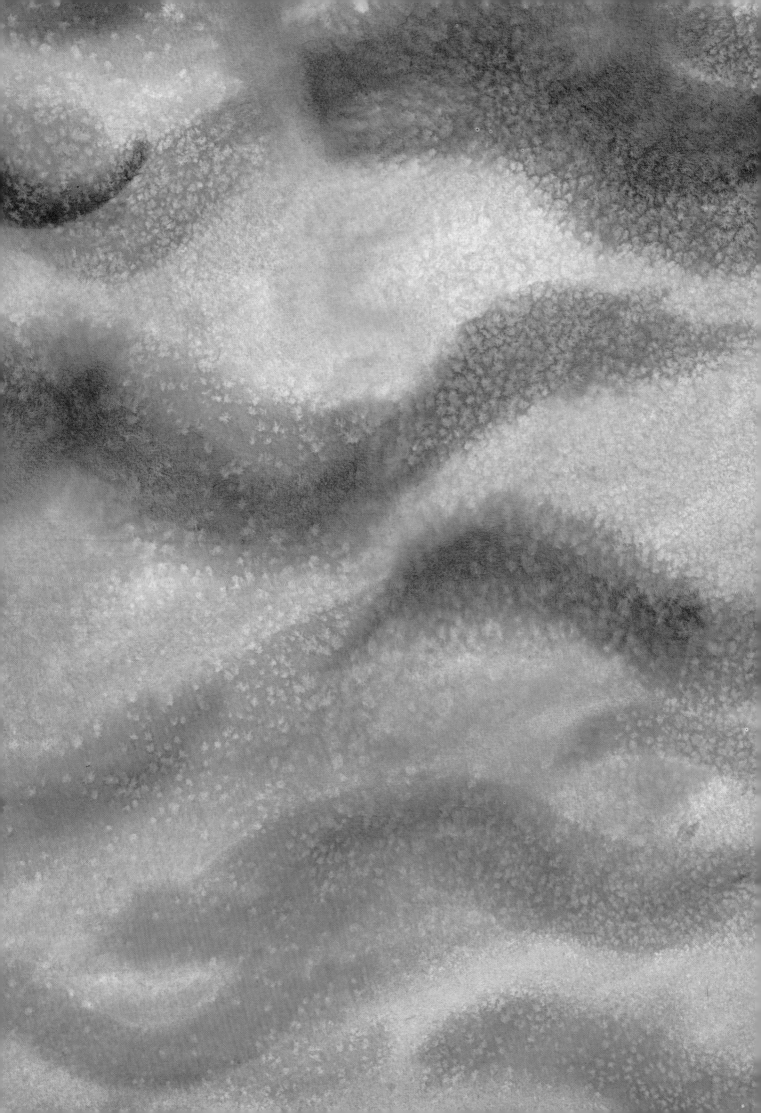